Karen's Chain Letter

Other books by
Ann M. Martin

P. S. Longer Letter Later
(written with Paula Danziger)
Leo the Magnificat
Rachel Parker, Kindergarten Show-off
Eleven Kids, One Summer
Ma and Pa Dracula
Yours Turly, Shirley
Ten Kids, No Pets
With You and Without You
Me and Katie (the Pest)
Stage Fright
Inside Out
Bummer Summer

For older readers:

Missing Since Monday
Just a Summer Romance
Slam Book

THE BABY-SITTERS CLUB series
THE BABY-SITTERS CLUB mysteries
THE KIDS IN MS. COLMAN'S CLASS series
BABY-SITTERS LITTLE SISTER series
(see inside book covers for a complete listing)

Little Sister

Karen's Chain Letter

Ann M. Martin

Illustrations by Susan Crocca Tang

SCHOLASTIC INC.
New York Toronto London Auckland Sydney

ISBN 0-590-50053-8

12 11 10 9 8 7 6 5 4 3 2 1 8 9/9 0 1 2 3/0

Printed in the U.S.A. 40

First Scholastic printing, September 1998

The author gratefully acknowledges
Jan Carr
for her help
with this book.

Karen's Chain Letter

A New Hobby

"Hello, Mr. Venta!" I called. "Is there any mail for me?"

Mr. Venta is our mail carrier. He and I are very good friends. Every day last month, I met him at the end of our driveway. He would hand the mail right to me. But now it was September and I had gone back to school so I did not see Mr. Venta every day. But that day I was lucky. When I got home from school, the mail had not arrived yet. So I watched for Mr. Venta's truck. When I saw it, I ran to meet him.

"I am sorry I am so late today, Karen," he said. He handed me a big stack of mail. None of the envelopes was addressed to me, but some had very pretty stamps on them.

"Any good ones?" asked Mr. Venta. I had told him all about my new hobby.

"Oh, yes," I said. "Thank you very much."

In case you have not guessed, my new hobby was stamp collecting. So far, I had collected stamps with birds on them and stamps with flowers and even stamps with dinosaurs. I had made a special album to keep them in. I had decorated each page with very beautiful pictures. I could not wait to glue these new stamps in. I waved good-bye to Mr. Venta and ran into the house with the mail. *Snip, snip.* I had to cut off the stamps very carefully.

"Karen," said a voice. Uh-oh. It was my daddy. He sounded a little angry. "What are you doing?"

"I am being very careful," I replied. "See? I

did not ruin the envelope or the letter inside."

Daddy took the envelope from me.

"This is business mail," he said. "You need to give it to me before you cut it up. I will give you the envelope when I finish with it. Remember? That is what we agreed."

"Oh," I said. Actually, I did not really remember any such thing. Sometimes it is easy for me to forget. Especially when I am working on an exciting new hobby.

Kristy came home then. She is my stepsister. "Is that the mail?" she asked. She picked up the stack and sorted through it. "A letter from Michel!" she cried.

Michel lives in Toronto. He is Kristy's new friend, and he writes her all the time. This is lucky for me, because Toronto is in Canada, which is a whole different country. So Michel's letters always have Canadian stamps on them. Kristy tore open the envelope and turned toward the door.

"Hey," I cried. "Can I have the stamp?"

"Later," said Kristy.

"Please?" I begged.

Kristy sighed. "All right." She tore off the stamp and handed it to me. "Did you get any mail from Chicago?" she asked.

"Not today," I said.

"Maybe tomorrow, then. I bet Andrew will draw you a picture and send it. You know he misses you."

Andrew is my little brother. He and my mother and my stepfather, Seth, were living in Chicago for a few months. Usually, Andrew and I switch houses together every month. One month we live with Mommy's family at the little house, and the next month we live with Daddy's family at the big house. But these months were different. Andrew had gone to Chicago, and I had decided to stay with my big-house family here in Stoneybrook, Connecticut. My little-house family would not return to Stoneybrook for two more months.

Oops. Maybe you do not know anything about my two families or my two houses. Do not worry. I will tell you all about them. There is so much to tell!

Two Great Families

Let me start at the beginning. My name is Karen Brewer. I have blonde hair and blue eyes and freckles. I wear glasses. I have a blue pair for reading and a pink pair for the rest of the time. They make me look very grown-up. I am in second grade and I live with my two families in Stoneybrook, Connecticut.

I did not always have two families. A long time ago, Andrew and Mommy and Daddy and I all lived together in the big house. At first Mommy and Daddy were happy, but then they started to fight a lot. And one day they told us they were going to get a divorce. Daddy stayed in the big house, which is the house he grew up in. And Mommy moved to a little house that was not too far away.

After awhile, Mommy met a man named Seth and they got married. Seth is my stepfather. He is gigundoly nice. He has a dog named Midgie and a cat named Rocky, and now they live in the little house too. So do Emily Junior, my pet rat, and Bob, Andrew's hermit crab. (Actually, Emily Junior and Bob go wherever we go.)

Now I will tell you about the big house. Daddy got married again too. He married a really nice woman named Elizabeth, who is my stepmother. She already had four children. So now I have three stepbrothers and a stepsister. Sam and Charlie are the oldest. They are cool high school guys. Then there is Kristy. She is thirteen and the best stepsister ever. David Michael is seven, like me, but he goes to a different school.

And those are not the only people in the big house. I have one more sister, Emily Michelle. Daddy and Elizabeth adopted her from a faraway country called Vietnam. And finally there is Nannie. She is Elizabeth's mother. She came to live with us so she could help take care of Emily Michelle, which is a big job because Emily Michelle gets into everything. (She is only two and a half.)

Now I will tell you about the big-house pets. Right now we have two dogs. David Michael has a Bernese mountain dog puppy named Shannon, and Kristy is helping to train a Labrador puppy named Scout. She is going to be a guide dog for the blind! We also have a cat, Daddy's old cat Boo-Boo, and two goldfish. I have one named Crystal Light the Second and Andrew has one he named . . . guess what? Goldfishie.

"Do you miss them?" asked Kristy.

"The goldfish?" I asked. "Why would I miss them? They are here."

Kristy looked confused. Oops. I guess she

was not talking about my goldfish. That's right. We were talking about my little-house family.

"I miss them a lot," I said.

Then I looked at the stamp Kristy had given me. Wow! Not only was it from Canada, it was a stamp of Winnie-the-Pooh.

Dingdong. Someone had rung the doorbell. I ran to answer it. It was Mr. Venta.

"Hi, Karen," he said. "I found another letter for you at the bottom of my bag. It must have gotten separated from your pack."

I looked at the letter. It was from Chicago. And it was addressed to me! I tore open the envelope. Inside was a picture Andrew had drawn (Kristy was right), and a note from Mommy. Something fell out of the note and fluttered to the floor. Stamps!

I saved these stamps for you, Mommy wrote. *I hope you like them. I miss you, honey. We cannot wait to see you when we get back in November.*

I could not wait to see Mommy and Seth and Andrew. I really missed them too.

I picked up the stamps off the floor. Wow! One had a picture of a carousel horse on it, and another had a picture of an opera singer.

"Thanks, Mr. Venta," I said. I held my hand high and slapped him five. "And if you happen to find any *stamps* loose at the bottom of your bag, you can bring them to me. I know just what to do with them."

The Chain Letter

When you are a stamp collector, you think about the stamps you have. You also think about how you can get *more* stamps. Every day you hope that someone will send you some really good stamps in the mail.

The next day in school I was thinking about my collection. I was thinking it would be great if someone would send me a letter from Australia. Then I would have a stamp from all the way around the world. I figured that an Australian stamp would probably have a kangaroo on it. I imagined how it would look in my album.

"Karen?" said Ms. Colman. Ms. Colman is my teacher. She was standing over me. She was staring at me, as if she expected me to say something.

"Yes?" I said.

"I just asked you a question."

"Oh." This was embarrassing. "I guess I did not hear you."

Ms. Colman laughed. She is a gigundoly nice teacher. I think she must be the best teacher in the entire world.

"You did look deep in thought," she said. "May I ask what you were thinking about?"

"Stamps," I replied.

"Stamps?"

"Yes. I am a stamp collector now. That is my new hobby."

"How interesting," said Ms. Colman. "Maybe you could bring in your collection to show the class."

"Okay," I said. "Maybe next week."

If I was going to show my stamp album to

the class, I would need to fix it up so it would be perfect. It would be nice to add a few more really special stamps. Maybe some from overseas. There was only one problem. How was I going to come up with better stamps so quickly?

At home that afternoon, I found a big surprise. Mr. Venta had already delivered the mail. On the top of the pile was another letter for me. The envelope had a regular old flag stamp. Boo. I already had plenty of those. But the letter was from Maxie, my pen pal in New York City. I ran to my room to read the letter. It was a chain letter! I had heard of chain letters, but I had never gotten one before.

Dear Karen, I read. *This is a good-luck chain letter. I got it from someone who got it from someone at Kidsnetwork. (That is a group that plans fun and safe activities for kids.) If you follow the directions and send this letter to other kids within three days, your luck will get better and better.*

Well. Usually I have very good luck. But a

person can always use more. To get more stamps, for one thing.

I continued reading the letter. It spelled out all the things I needed to do. It told me to retype the letter, add my name and address to a small list of names at the bottom, and remove the name and address at the top of the list. Then I was supposed to send the letter to ten other kids. I knew right away who two of them would be. I would send one letter each to Hannie and Nancy. They are my absolute best friends. Then, after I sent out the letters, I should mail a postcard to the person whose name had been at the top of the list. The letter promised that if I did, I would receive postcards in the mail too. Lots of them.

Postcards? That could only mean one thing — more stamps! My luck was improving already. This was going to be fun.

"Hey," said Kristy. She poked her head around the door of my room. She was zipping up her sweatshirt. "I am going to go

into town with Charlie," she said. "Do you want to come?"

"Sure," I answered. I jumped off my bed. "I have to buy something."

"What?"

"A postcard."

"Oh yeah?" asked Kristy. "What for?"

"It's a secret," I said mysteriously.

Soon lots of postcards addressed to me would start arriving in our mail. Then I would tell Kristy everything. She would be *very* surprised!

The Three Musketeers

The next day at recess I told Hannie and Nancy about the chain letter.

"I already bought the postcard I will send," I said. "It is a beautiful picture of the Stoneybrook Arboretum."

"Did you send out the letters to the ten people yet?" Nancy asked.

"No," I said. "I will do that this afternoon, after school."

"Are you going to send one to me?" she asked.

"And me?" Hannie chimed in.

"Well, of course I will. You are my best friends. We are the Three Musketeers."

We linked our pinkies and squeezed them tightly.

"And anyway," I told my friends, "I want you both to have good luck. Just like me."

"Then I will ask my mom's permission right after school," said Nancy.

"Me too," said Hannie.

"Permission?" I said. "For what?"

"To answer the chain letter," said Nancy.

I had not thought of that. I had not asked anyone's permission, but I was sure Daddy would think it was okay. After all, Maxie said the letter came from Kidsnetwork.

I pulled a small bag out of my pocket.

"And now," I said, "I will show you some of the new stamps I have collected."

I laid the stamps out neatly in a row so Hannie and Nancy could see them. Some other kids gathered around. Addie Sidney came, and so did Pamela Harding. Soon the whole class was bunched around me. Everyone wanted to see the stamps.

"Where did they all come from?" asked Nancy. She seemed especially impressed.

"Different places," I said. "Nannie has a chocolate business, and a lot of her orders come by mail. Nannie and Daddy get tons of important mail. And Kristy has friends she writes to in England and Canada. And college brochures come for Charlie. Plus Mommy and Seth and Andrew send me mail from Chicago."

"All right, all right," Pamela cut me off. "We get the picture."

I made a face at Pamela. I think I forgot to tell you that Pamela is my best enemy. Sometimes she can be a real meanie-mo.

Nancy picked up one of the stamps and looked at it more closely. "I never knew that stamps could be so cool," she said.

Just then, the bell rang and everyone started lining up to file back into school. Recess was over.

"Musketeers," I whispered to Hannie and Nancy as we crowded into line, "do not forget to watch for your mail."

Inside the classroom, I took my seat and looked at the clock. I wished the school day would go faster. Time was ticking. I wanted to be at home, retyping the chain letter. I had only two days left to send it out.

A New Address

I did not realize how long it would take to type a whole letter. After school, I hurried to eat the snack Nannie had fixed (it was Rice Krispies treats). Then I went straight to our family computer and turned it on. I typed the whole letter. At the end, I added my own name and address. Then I printed out ten copies. Now all I needed were some envelopes and stamps. I went to Daddy's office and knocked on his door. He always lets me use his supplies.

"What do you need, pumpkin?" Daddy asked.

"Just some envelopes and stamps, please."

"How many?" he asked. He pulled a pack of envelopes out of the drawer.

"Ten," I said.

"Ten?" said Daddy. "What in the world are you mailing?"

"My chain letter," I replied. I handed him a copy. I was sure Daddy would think it was cool. Sometimes, though, Daddy surprises me. As he read the letter, his face grew very serious.

"I am sorry, Karen," he said when he finished, "but I cannot let you send this out." He handed the letter back to me.

"What?" I cried. "Why not?" Maybe there was something he did not understand.

"First of all," said Daddy, "it is against the law to send some chain letters through the mail. The post office keeps track of these things. If you send a chain letter that tells people to send money, you can be arrested."

Arrested! I had no idea that something that was as much fun as a chain letter could be so much trouble.

"But my letter does not ask people to send money," I said. "Look. It says to send a *postcard.*"

"Well, there is another problem," said Daddy. "I do not want you sending your name and address to strangers."

"I am not sending it to strangers," I said patiently. "I am sending it to Hannie and Nancy and other people I know. All my friends already know my name and address."

"Yes, but Hannie and Nancy will send the letter out to others, and then those people will send it out too, and soon it will be going to people we have never heard of. In the end, we have no control over where this letter will go."

It seemed to me that that was the fun part. How else was I going to get a postcard from Australia?

"Daddy," I said, "this chain letter comes

from Kidsnetwork. It will only be sent to other kids."

"I am sorry, Karen," said Daddy. "The answer is no. If it were part of a school project, I would feel different. But you will have to go along with me on this. I am your father and it is my job to look out for your safety."

Daddy turned back to his work. I could not believe this had happened. This was a problem. A big problem. But the good thing about problems is that they usually have solutions. If you think hard enough, you can figure them out.

Daddy had said that if the letter were part of a school project, he would feel different. That gave me an idea. If he did not want me to send out my home address, maybe I could send out the school's address. That was it! Perfect. I sat down at the computer again. I took my street address off the bottom of the letter. In its place, I typed, *Karen Brewer, c/o Ms. Colman's class, Stoneybrook Academy.* I crumpled up the old letters and printed out ten copies of the new one.

Now all I had to do was mail them. I found some stamps in a drawer in the kitchen. There were only eight, but I did not want to bother Daddy again. He seemed to be in a very cranky mood. I thought of a solution to that problem too, though. The next day at school I could hand Hannie and Nancy their letters in person.

"Congratulations, Karen Brewer," I said to myself.

I had solved all of my problems. Daddy always tells me to use my noodle. I was sure that if he knew how many problems I had solved, he would be very proud of my noodle indeed.

Hannie's Mistake

The next day was Friday. Before I left for school, I folded up the letters I had saved for Hannie and Nancy and put them in my backpack. I waited until we were together in our classroom. Then I handed the letters to my friends. I stood between them as they read their copies. I pointed out the important parts, in case Hannie and Nancy missed them.

"See," I said. "It says you have to send out ten letters."

"Mmm," said Hannie.

"But you have to send them to kids only. And after that you have to send a postcard to the person at the top of the list."

"You told us that the other day," said Nancy.

"But the most important thing," I continued, ignoring her, "is that you have to do all of this in three days."

"Karen," Nancy snapped at me, "we can read."

"I am only trying to help," I said. "Since I am the one sending you the letter, it is my responsibility to make sure you understand it. I certainly do not want you to do anything that would cause you bad luck."

Nancy rolled her eyes, but Hannie nodded solemnly. "Three days," she repeated.

At least one of my friends seemed to understand the importance of what I was saying.

The next day was Saturday. I had a lot to do. I had decided to work on my stamp album so that it would look perfect when I brought it in to show the class. In the afternoon, I called Nancy. I asked her if she had sent out the letter yet.

"I am typing it right now," she said. "Do you want to come over and make sure I am doing it right?"

Nancy did not sound as if she really meant that. Sometimes people do not understand when you are trying to help them.

After that, I went over to Hannie's house to play. I helped her with her letters. It took all afternoon. That night, I called her on the phone.

"Did you address the envelopes yet?" I asked.

"Oh, yeah," Hannie said when I reminded her. "The envelopes. I will try to address them tomorrow."

Hmm. It sounded almost as if she had forgotten. The next morning I went over to her house bright and early to make sure that she remembered. I helped her address the envelopes. We worked very carefully.

"There," I said when we were finished. I thought my work was done.

But Monday morning when we were on the school bus, I found out I was wrong.

"Did you mail the letters?" I asked.

I was heading down the aisle, looking for a seat. Hannie was behind me.

"Not yet," she answered. "Mommy said she would take them to the post office this afternoon."

"This afternoon!" I cried. "That is too late. Your three days are up this morning!"

Hannie's face turned pale. "No, they are not," she said. "I have until tomorrow, don't I?"

"I gave the letter to you on Friday morning," I said. "Count the days from Friday morning. Saturday, Sunday, Monday morning. That is three. I thought you were going to mail them out yesterday after you typed them!"

"We did not have enough stamps," said Hannie. "And the post office is closed on Sunday."

I tossed my backpack on a seat and sat down. Hannie slid in beside me. Obviously, Hannie was not as good at solving problems as I was. The bus pulled down the street. It was too late to do anything. We were heading toward school. Away from Hannie's house. Away from the unmailed letters.

"Do you think I will have really bad luck?" Hannie asked.

I did not know what to say. Of course she would have bad luck. "I hope not," I told her.

"How is a person supposed to mail a letter if she does not have any stamps?" Hannie asked crossly. She thought for a moment. "Maybe Sunday did not really count," she said. "Because of the post office being closed and all."

"Maybe," I said. I did not think so, but I did not want Hannie to worry.

"This is terrible," Hannie said. "Now I will have bad luck. Really bad luck."

I was afraid Hannie was right. And I

knew it was partly my fault. I should have called her again on Sunday night, but I had been too busy working on my stamp album. How had everything gone so wrong? Where was my good luck?

Show-and-Share

At school I did not spend much more time worrying about Hannie. I had other important things to do. I opened my backpack and peeked in. Yup. There it was, sandwiched safely between my book and my notebook. I had worked very hard on my stamp album. Finally it was ready for everyone to see.

Soon Ms. Colman announced it was time for show-and-share. "Does anyone have anything to show us today?" she asked. My heart started pounding. I almost shouted out, but just in time I clapped my hand over my mouth and remembered to raise my hand.

Ms. Colman smiled. "Yes, Karen?" she said.

"Today," I said when I reached the front of the room, "I have brought in something very special. It is the stamp collection I told you about last week." I held the album high so everyone could see. I had decorated the cover with red and gold glitter.

"Ooh!" someone cried out.

"As you can see," I continued, "my album is very beautiful. But the important things are the stamps inside." I opened the book. In the center of the first page was a stamp with a picture of a red flower. On the page around it, I had drawn lots of red bouquets.

"Every year," I told my classmates, "the post office prints stamps with different pictures on them. They are called special-issue stamps." I turned the pages of my album — slowly, carefully — so the class could see all the different stamps I had collected.

"If you are a stamp collector, you can also collect stamps from different countries," I said. By this time I was turning the last, most impressive, pages of my book. "I am lucky, because my big sister, Kristy, gets mail from other countries. As you can see, these Canadian stamps are very colorful."

And now I had reached the last page. On it was a stamp from England. "This stamp is the queen," I said. "The queen of England. If you grow up to be a famous person like the queen, you might be important enough to have your picture on a stamp."

When I had finished, lots of hands shot up. My classmates had plenty of questions.

"How do you take the stamps off the envelopes?" asked Sara Ford.

"I cut them off with scissors," I said. "You have to be very careful not to nick the stamps."

"And how do you put them on the page?" asked Addie.

"Glue," I answered. "Regular glue."

"Thank you, Karen," said Ms. Colman

when I had answered all the questions. "That was very interesting."

"I forgot one thing," I added quickly. "If anyone would like to start a stamp collection, please feel free to ask me any question anytime."

"That is very generous of you," said Ms. Colman. Then she called on the next person who had something to talk about.

I cannot say that I paid much attention. I was still glowing from my own talk. I was very proud of my stamp collection and all the work I had done. Soon, I thought, lots of postcards would start rolling in from the chain letter I had sent. Each one would have a stamp. And then my collection would be even better.

I counted back the days in my head to Thursday. That was the day I had mailed out the chain letter. I knew it was too early to expect any postcards yet, but I wondered when they would start to arrive. Tomorrow maybe? The next day? How long would I have to wait before my good luck began?

One thing was certain. It was very lucky that I had written the school address on my letter. Lucky for my classmates. Now they would be able to see all my beautiful new stamps as soon as they arrived.

Waiting for Mail

The next morning when the bus dropped Hannie and me off at school, I decided not to go straight to my classroom. I walked past the school office and waved to Ms. Agna, the secretary. I figured that if any mail for me had been delivered to the office, she would be the first person to know.

"Hello, Ms. Agna," I said. "That is a very pretty dress." It was true. Her dress had big pictures of teapots printed on it. Ms. Agna always wears cool clothes.

"Thank you," she said. But she did not say anything about any mail.

The next morning I walked by the office again. This time I stopped and talked a bit longer.

"I do not know if you remember me from last year," I said, "but my name is Karen Brewer." I reached out and shook Ms. Agna's hand. She looked a little surprised.

"I am glad to meet you, Karen," she said.

"I am in Ms. Colman's second grade," I said. "If you need me for any reason, you can find me there. For instance, if any mail arrives for me."

"I will remember that," she said. Then the phone rang and she answered it. I hurried off to class.

Every morning that week I stopped to talk to Ms. Agna. Never once did she say anything to me about any mail. And that was not the only thing that worried me. In class all my friends had started talking about stamps. Stamps, stamps, and more stamps. I was not the only stamp collector in the class anymore. Nancy announced that she had started a collection. Hannie had started one too. Then Pamela started one, then Addie, and Ricky Torres, and Terri and Tammy Barkan. Each day at show-and-share, someone new brought in stamps to show. And then I noticed something terrible. Lots of kids were bringing in stamps that were better than mine.

"Look what I have," Nancy said to me one day on the playground. She fished in her pocket and pulled out an envelope. She picked out some stamps and laid them across her palm. She had queen stamps from England! They were just like the one I had, only Nancy had four of them and they were all different colors!

"Stamps from other countries are very cool," said Nancy. "My uncle does a lot of traveling for his work and he gets mail from all over the world."

"No fair," I muttered.

"What?" said Nancy.

"Nothing," I said quickly. I knew I had

sounded like a meanie-mo, but I could not help it. Stamp collecting was *my* hobby, *my* idea. Everyone else in the class was being a copycat. Copycats with better stamps. If only my postcards would start coming in. Then my good-luck streak would finally start, and my collection would be the best again.

Well, until that happened, I would just have to work a little harder. After school that day, I talked to the people in my family.

"Kristy," I began, "have you written your friends who live in other countries lately? They will not write to you if you do not write them first."

Kristy grinned. "You need some more stamps, don't you?" she asked.

"How did you know?"

"Just a guess."

"Well, if you write any of your friends in England, could you please ask them to send queen stamps?" I said. "Ones with different colors?"

"I will," said Kristy. "When I have a chance to write."

That did not sound too promising.

Next, I tracked down Nannie. I was hoping she might have received some interesting mail. But some of her customers had begun sending their orders by fax. That meant no stamps. I decided to talk to Nannie about this problem.

"Nannie," I said, "I do not think it is good that some of your customers have started faxing their orders to you. I am a little bit worried about the post office. How will they ever stay in business if nobody sends mail anymore?"

Nannie laughed. "I cannot ask my customers to stop using the fax," she said. "But I know you need stamps, Karen. So I saved you this envelope that came in today's mail."

Nannie handed me an envelope with lots of stamps on it. Some were for five cents, some were for ten cents, and some were for one cent. Together, they all added up to the price of a regular stamp. I had not seen any stamps like that before. They were kind of cool.

"Gee, thanks, Nannie," I said.

I ran to my room to glue the new stamps in my album. Maybe this was the beginning of my good-luck streak!

Bales of Mail

Finally, on Friday, I had a big surprise. I was in class and we were reading silently. Ms. Colman had said we could find comfortable reading seats so I had flopped down on one of the big, fluffy pillows in our reading corner. Hannie was sitting beside me. She leaned over and whispered in my ear, "She has the coolest clothes of any grown-up I know."

"Who?" I asked.

Hannie pointed. Oh, my gosh! Ms. Agna was standing in our doorway talking to Ms.

Colman. In her arms she held a plastic sack.

"Karen?" said Ms. Colman. She motioned to me. I ran to her and she held the sack open for me to look inside. "Apparently you have received some mail at school," she said.

"My postcards!" I cried. "From my chain letter."

"Chain letter?" repeated Ms. Colman.

"Yes," I said. "It is sponsored by Kidsnetwork. These are postcards from all over the world!"

"Well," said Ms. Colman, "I can see that you are very excited. Perhaps you could share some of the postcards with the rest of the class."

Ms. Agna left, and Ms. Colman sorted through the cards and picked out one for me to read aloud. It was from a girl who lived on an island near Seattle. She had to ride on a ferryboat every day to go to school. "How do you get to school?" she asked. At the bottom of the postcard she had printed her name and address, so I could write back.

I did not read any more of the postcards

then, though. Ms. Colman took the bag and kept it at her desk. When it was time for lunch and recess, she handed the bag to me. "You might want to look at them outside," she suggested.

Later, on the playground, everyone crowded around.

"Is that a horse stamp?" asked Pamela. She grabbed a postcard out of the sack.

It was not a horse stamp. It was a regular old postcard stamp. Oh no. I had forgotten about postcard stamps. There are not as many kinds. So they are usually not as interesting as letter stamps. I looked through the bag quickly. Good. Not all of the cards had postcard stamps. Some had letter stamps. Pamela grabbed another card out of the bag.

"Here is a horse stamp," she said.

Nancy reached in too. "And here are two more," she said. "Hey, you have so many. Would you share some of them? Please?"

Everyone was staring at me. I would look like a meanie-mo if I did not say yes. "Okay," I said. I tore off two stamps and

gave one to Nancy and one to Pamela. "But the rest are all mine," I said. "And everyone is crowding me. Could you please stand back?" I closed up the bag tightly. Maybe it would be better to look through the cards later, when I was alone.

Across the yard, some kids from another class were playing keep-away. I ran to join them. The bag bumped against my stomach. I thought of all the cards inside. Even though some of the stamps were postcard stamps, there were sure to be lots of wonderful letter stamps too. My good-luck streak was definitely beginning. It had started when I spotted Ms. Agna standing in our door.

I ran past Ms. Colman. She was talking to another teacher.

"Oh, Karen," she called to me. "I would like to speak with you, please. In the classroom. Alone."

Alone? Uh-oh. That could only mean trouble. I slung my bag over my shoulder and waved to Hannie and Nancy so they would know I was leaving. My friends watched me as I followed Ms. Colman back into school. What could the problem be now?

Trouble

As soon as we were inside the classroom, Ms. Colman closed the door. Yikes. I wondered what she was going to ask me. She perched herself on a corner of her desk and folded her hands.

"I want to speak with you about the chain letter," she said. Oh. Was that all? "Did you know that some chain letters are against the law?" she asked.

"Oh, yes," I said quickly. "Do not worry about a thing. No one is going to be arrested. This chain letter is perfectly legal.

You only send postcards, not money. And you are only supposed to send it to kids."

"That may be so," said Ms. Colman. "But I would like you to bring in the letter so I can read it myself. And I have another question."

"You do?" I asked.

"Why are the postcards being mailed to you here at school?"

"Because I put the school address on the chain letter," I said.

"But why did you do that?"

"My daddy suggested it."

"Your father told you to use the school's address?"

"Yes. He thought it was not very safe for me to give out my home address to strangers. So he said it would be better if the postcards were delivered to me at school."

Ms. Colman tapped her fingers together thoughtfully. "Well," she said slowly, "I can see that your father has your safety at heart, but I am surprised that he did not call the school first to ask if it was okay. Children

are not supposed to receive mail here. Not unless it is part of a school project. It is too much work for the office to keep up with. And when our class is interrupted, it disrupts our important work."

Oh. I had not thought of that. And I guessed that Daddy had not either. Usually he is very good at keeping the rules of the school in mind. Maybe this time he just forgot.

There was a knock on the door. I knew it must be my classmates. Recess was over and they were ready to come back inside.

"Karen," said Ms. Colman, "after school I will need to call your father. The postcards will continue to come to our class. It is too late to stop them. But I want you and your father to understand the rules."

She walked to the door and opened it. Bobby Gianelli pushed through, and the other kids followed. Hannie and Nancy ran to me. I knew they wanted to find out what Ms. Colman had said. But I felt kind of funny. I was not the one in trouble, exactly.

It was Daddy. Still, I felt a little bit like I was in trouble too. This was all very confusing.

"Is everything okay?" asked Nancy.

"I guess so," I said.

I picked up the bag of postcards and stuffed it into my backpack. I was glad it was almost the weekend. I did not seem to be having very good luck at school. I thought that the chain letter Maxie had sent me was supposed to bring good luck. But so far, a lot of things were happening that were not one bit good at all.

More Mail

That afternoon, Daddy was waiting for me when I came home from school. His arms were crossed across his chest. I could tell he was angry.

"Karen," he said, "I hear that postcards are being delivered to you at school."

"Yes." I thought Daddy knew that already. I thought that was the plan.

"And Ms. Colman seems to think that I told you to have them sent there."

"Maybe you did not understand about the school rule," I replied.

"Oh, no," said Daddy. "I understand perfectly well about the rule. And I never told you to use the school address. When you showed me the chain letter, I told you that you were not allowed to send it out at all."

Hmm. I tried to think back. That is not the way I remembered it. "I thought you said I could answer the chain letter if it was part of a school project," I said.

"That is a far cry from telling you to use the school address without my permission," said Daddy.

Uh-oh. This was a misunderstanding. A big misunderstanding. I know about misunderstandings. Daddy and I have had them a few times before. I do not like them. They are not any fun at all.

"And now Ms. Colman is upset," Daddy continued. "And I cannot blame her. I would be upset too." Daddy was angry now. He was angry at *me.*

"I guess I heard wrong," I said. And then I added quickly, "I am sorry, Daddy."

"You must learn to listen more carefully,"

said Daddy. "All right, Karen. There will be no TV this weekend. Maybe that will help you remember to listen next time."

No TV? That did not seem fair to me. Why should I be punished for a little misunderstanding?

"How about if I tape the shows I want to see and watch them when my punishment is over?" I asked.

"Absolutely not," said Daddy.

Boo and bullfrogs. Daddy was being awfully strict. Oh, well. I guessed I did not really need to watch TV that weekend anyway. I could use the time to fix up my stamp album. I could make new pages. I would need more room for all the new stamps I would have now that my postcards had started to arrive. I wondered how many more would be at school on Monday. Maybe another bagful. Maybe even more.

On Monday, lots more postcards were waiting for me. Ms. Agna brought them to our class. I smiled and waved at her, but she did not smile back. Ms. Colman did not look happy either. They glanced at me and whispered in the doorway. Oh, dear. This time, Ms. Colman did not let me read any of the cards out loud. She put the bag away and did not say a word about it. When it was time for recess, she forgot to give it to me, so I had to remind her. Ms. Colman sighed.

"All right," she said. "But you need to put them in your cubby as soon as you come back inside. I do not want these postcards to disrupt our class."

Boo. Everybody certainly was touchy lately. I took the bag and followed my friends to the cafeteria. Later, on the playground, Pamela ran to me. When I opened the bag to look at the stamps, she tried to peer in. This time I was not going to let her.

"Hey," I said, "these are my cards."

"I do not know about that," Pamela said. "They were delivered to school. That means you have to share them. Including the stamps."

What? That was the craziest idea I had ever heard. I held a card up to her face.

"Look," I said. "The postcards have my name on them. That means they are mine."

Pamela grabbed the card out of my hand.

"Hey!" she said. "A waterfall stamp! Do you have two? If you do, you should give this one to me."

Boy oh boy, was I ever sorry I had shared any of my stamps with Pamela in the first place. If I gave her one of each double stamp that came, her collection would be better than mine in no time.

I grabbed the card.

"Find your own stamps," I said. "Stamp hog!"

Pamela ran off to complain to Ms. Colman, but I did not pay any attention. Sometimes Pamela can be the meanest of the meanie-mos. And I was sure Ms. Colman would take my side.

Rotten Luck

By this time my luck was pretty bad. I did not think it could get much worse. But the next day, when Ms. Agna came to our class with another bag of postcards, my luck went from bad to rotten.

I had already decided I did not want to take the postcards to recess with me. I would wait until the end of the day to ask Ms. Colman for them. Then I would tuck them in my backpack and leave them there until I got home. That way there would be no problems. That seemed like a very good plan.

But as soon as Ms. Agna left the room, Pamela started waving her hand.

"Yes, Pamela?" said Ms. Colman.

"I have a complaint to make," Pamela announced. "I do not think it is fair for Karen to get mail at school. Not unless she shares it. I think we should divide up the postcards and give some to everyone in the class."

Well, for heaven's sake! I waved my hand so Ms. Colman would call on me.

"The postcards are mine," I said. "I am sorry I ever had them delivered to school. But it would not be fair for anybody else to have them. The kids who wrote the cards wrote to *me*."

"You are the one who is hogging all the stamps!" Pamela shouted.

"Just a moment. Just a moment," said Ms. Colman. "These postcards have become a real problem. Let me think about this for a minute. There must be a solution."

Everyone in the class sat quietly, watching, waiting, as Ms. Colman thought. I sat the most quietly of all.

"I have an idea," she said after a minute. "I agree that the postcards themselves belong to Karen. But the stamps on the cards are a different matter. We can distribute them to anyone who is interested. Each day, when the postcards arrive, we will have a grab bag. Everyone may have a chance to reach into the bag and pull out one card. Then we will cut off the stamps and give the cards back to Karen."

I could not believe my ears. Usually, Ms. Colman is a very fair teacher. But this was not fair at all. I raised my hand to protest, but Ms. Colman did not call on me. Instead, she held the bag out in front of her.

"Karen," she said, "you may be the first to choose a stamp."

Ms. Colman looked as if she had made up her mind. I guessed I did not have much choice. I walked to Ms. Colman's desk and reached into the bag. I certainly did not want to take the first card I touched. It might be one of those cards you can buy at the post office, the kind that have the stamps already printed on them. I felt around for a real postcard with a real stamp. I wanted a big stamp. That would mean it would be one with a good picture, not a regular old flag stamp or a postcard stamp. When I felt a big stamp I pulled out the card. Boo and bullfrogs. It was a horse stamp, the kind I had given Pamela and Nancy last week on the playground.

Next, Ms. Colman told Pamela she could choose a card from the bag. Pamela smiled a meanie-mo smile as she walked past me. She reached into the bag and pulled out a card. Oh no! It had a really cool stamp with a picture of a famous movie star on it. I had been hoping for one of those.

"Thank you, Ms. Colman," Pamela said sweetly.

But that was not the only bad thing to happen that day. Later, when we went to the playground, Pamela followed Hannie and Nancy and me as if she had something more to say. I spun around and snapped at her.

"Listen, I do not have any more stamps. You already took the best one. So there is no reason for you to follow me around today, is there?"

"I just wanted to thank you," said Pamela. "And I wanted to let you know that if I get any doubles of the movie star stamp, maybe I will give one to you. I will probably get lots of doubles when my postcards start coming in."

"What do you mean, 'your postcards'?" I asked.

"From my chain letter. Nancy sent a copy to Addie, and Addie sent one to me."

I looked at Nancy. She shrugged. I knew Nancy had not thought that Addie would send one of her letters to Pamela.

"So I should be receiving my postcards any day now," said Pamela. "Only *my* cards will be sent to my house. So I will not have to share them."

This was something I had not thought of. Other kids in the class had gotten the chain letter. If their parents had given them permission to send it out, then they would be getting their own postcards. With their own stamps. And all of theirs would be delivered straight to their houses.

"Thanks again," chirped Pamela. She ran off to join her friends.

Nancy reached into her pocket.

"Want to see my new stamps?" she asked.

I did not. "Who cares about stamps?" I said.

I stomped off to play by myself. Soon, my stamp collection would be the worst in the class by far.

Stamp Champ

The next day for show-and-share Nancy brought in her stamps. Her collection had grown big, much bigger than mine. She also brought in a magazine about stamp collecting. It was written especially for kids.

"On this page," she said, holding the magazine high, "it shows the correct way to take stamps off envelopes."

Hannie glanced at me. I knew what she was thinking. If Nancy's way was the correct way, then the way I had shown must be wrong.

Nancy set a bowl of warm water on Ms. Colman's desk to demonstrate. She cut a stamp off of an envelope, then dropped it into the water to soak. As we watched, the stamp came loose from the paper it was stuck on. Nancy fished the stamp out of the water with a special pair of tongs.

"This way," she said, "the stamp does not get damaged." She held up the dripping stamp. "When it is dry, you stick it in your album with one of these special mounts." She passed around a little gummed sticker for everyone to see. It had a special plastic window to protect the stamp. "You lick the back of it and stick it on the page," she said. "So it does not ruin the stamp, the way glue does."

After that, Ms. Colman called on Addie. Addie had brought in stamps too. She had organized hers in an album she had bought at the store. Personally, I liked my album much better. I think it takes much more creativity to make something beautiful yourself.

Hank Reubens was next. And what do you think he brought to show? Stamps. Well, for goodness sake. I did not know that Hank was interested in stamps too. It looked as if everyone in the class had started a collection now. Hank did not keep his stamps in an album, though. He had mounted his on trading cards.

"You can buy the cards at the post office," he said. "They are specially made for stamps. And by the way, I am interested in trading cards with anyone else. I am especially interested in basketball stamps. I would gladly trade my Joe Hunter for a Moose Mueller."

"Thank you, Hank," said Ms. Colman. "But I would rather that you save any trading for after school."

When show-and-share was finally over, Nancy ran to Hannie and me. She was so excited that she was practically bubbling over.

"Do you think everybody liked my demonstration?" she asked. "I thought it up last night while I was lying in bed. I knew it would be cool."

"It was all right," I said.

Nancy turned to Hannie. "Have you started a stamp collection yet?" she asked.

"Yes," Hannie said glumly, "but it is not going very well. I am not getting many postcards from my chain letter. And nobody sends my family any interesting stamps."

"How is your collection?" Nancy asked me.

"It is coming along very nicely, thank you," I said. I did not want to talk about stamps with Nancy, though she did not seem to notice. She grabbed my hand and squeezed it excitedly.

"Thanks, Karen," she said. "The chain letter really *did* bring me good luck. I think my collection might be the best in the class now. You guys can call me the Stamp Champ!"

Oh, brother.

That afternoon on the school bus, Hannie and I tried to figure out what went wrong.

"We knew that *you* would probably have

bad luck," I said to Hannie. "After all, you missed the deadline. But why am I having bad luck?"

"Did you mail all the letters on time?" asked Hannie.

"Of course," I said.

"Wait a minute," said Hannie. "You may have *given* them out on time, but you did not *mail* all of them."

"What do you mean?"

"Remember? You *handed* Nancy and me our letters. Maybe they were supposed to go through the mail."

I tried to think back to the chain letter. I could not remember if it had said anything specific about how the letters were supposed to be sent.

"Do you think that is the problem?" I asked.

"There must be an explanation," said Hannie. "What else could it be?"

I was not sure Hannie was right, but one thing was certain. My luck was now worse than rotten. It was lousy. I thought back to the day I had mailed the letters. If only we had had more stamps. Two measly more stamps would have cost less than a dollar. And now I was paying a big, big price.

Stamp Stampede

The next day's show-and-share was more of the same. Every single person except for Hannie and me brought in their stamps to show. And everyone tried to talk at once.

"Whoa!" cried Ms. Colman. "This feels like a stamp stampede!"

I could tell that Ms. Colman was a little tired of stamps. After five people had shared their collections, she made a suggestion. "I wonder if anyone has anything *else* to talk about? Does anyone have anything to share that is not about stamps?"

For a moment, no one spoke. Then Ricky Torres raised his hand.

"I have something to say," he began. "It is not exactly about stamps, but it is about a postcard I received because of the chain letter. Is that okay?"

"That sounds interesting," said Ms. Colman. "Go ahead."

Ricky held up his postcard. On the front was a picture of a baseball stadium. Ricky read the card. *Hi,* it said. *Here is a picture of Riverfront Stadium in Cincinnati. Sometimes I get to sit in the dugout. That is because my dad plays on the team. Please write back. Your friend, Armando Rivera.*

Ricky looked at us. "Armando *Rivera,*" he said. "Get it?"

We all just stared at him. I could not imagine what Ricky wanted us to get.

"His last name is Rivera," said Ricky. "It says his father plays on the team. That must mean his father is *José* Rivera. He plays for the Cincinnati Reds."

Wow! If Ricky was right, that was pretty cool.

"Good detective work, Ricky," said Ms. Colman. "And your postcard gives me an idea. I wonder if anyone else has an interesting card they want to read to the class."

At first no one said a word. The truth was, not many of us had bothered to read our postcards. We had been too busy thinking about the stamps. But some kids had a few cards in their desks. The room was quiet while they took out their cards and read them. Then Tammy Barkan raised her hand.

"This one is kind of interesting," she said. "It is from a girl who is training to be a figure skater. She lives in Minnesota. Look. She included her address too. She wants me to write back."

Then Natalie Springer showed us one of her postcards. It was homemade. The picture on the front was a photo that had been glued onto a piece of cardboard. The photo showed a girl riding a horse. *I like to ride horses,* the girl had written on the back. *I am learning how to jump.* This girl had included her address too.

Ms. Colman smiled. "Did you realize that so many of the kids who wrote you wanted you to respond?" she asked.

And then she told us her idea. "I think this might make an excellent writing project for us. Would you like to write back to the kids who put their return addresses on their postcards?"

"Like pen pals!" I shouted out.

"Exactly, Karen," she said. "Though please try to remember to raise your hand."

I was not the only one who thought Ms. Colman's idea was great. Bobby asked Ricky if he could write to the boy whose father was a baseball player. And Jannie Gilbert wanted to write to the girl who was learning to ride horses.

"I want everyone to bring in the postcards with return addresses," Ms. Colman told us. "You will also need to bring in permission notes from your parents saying that you may write to your pen pals and letting me know whether you may include your name and address. We will put all the postcards together in a big basket. Then, when we have had a chance to read through them, we will have Postcard Day. On that day, we will write letters to as many of our new friends as we can."

I raised my hand. "One question," I said. "When is Postcard Day?"

"How about Tuesday?" Ms. Colman replied.

"Hurrah!" I shouted. Oops. I was just so excited. Postcard Day was going to be great!

Cards in a Basket

The days leading up to Postcard Day were lots of fun. Ms. Colman brought in a big red basket. When we put our postcards in it, it was filled to the brim. I found lots of cards from kids I wanted to write back to. I even started composing a letter in my head. *My name is Karen Brewer,* it would begin. *And you might be interested to know that I was the very first kid in our class to receive the chain letter in the mail. I sent it to my friends, and they sent it to you.*

Wow! That made me realize something.

Our project had started because of me.

That is what I told Daddy when I asked him to write my permission note.

"No," he joked. "It was not because of you. It was me. Remember? I was the one who suggested that the chain letter be a class project. Or so I heard. From a certain daughter of mine with a very active imagination."

"Oh, Daddy," I said. I poked him in the arm. Sometimes my daddy can be just plain silly.

On Monday, Ms. Colman posted a big map, and we spent the morning looking at the postcards to find out where they were from. We discovered that we had postcards from thirty-four of the fifty states.

Ms. Colman had brought in some push pins with brightly colored tops. "Karen," she said, "would you like to come up front and stick the pins into the right states on the map?"

"Sure," I said. I am excellent at geography.

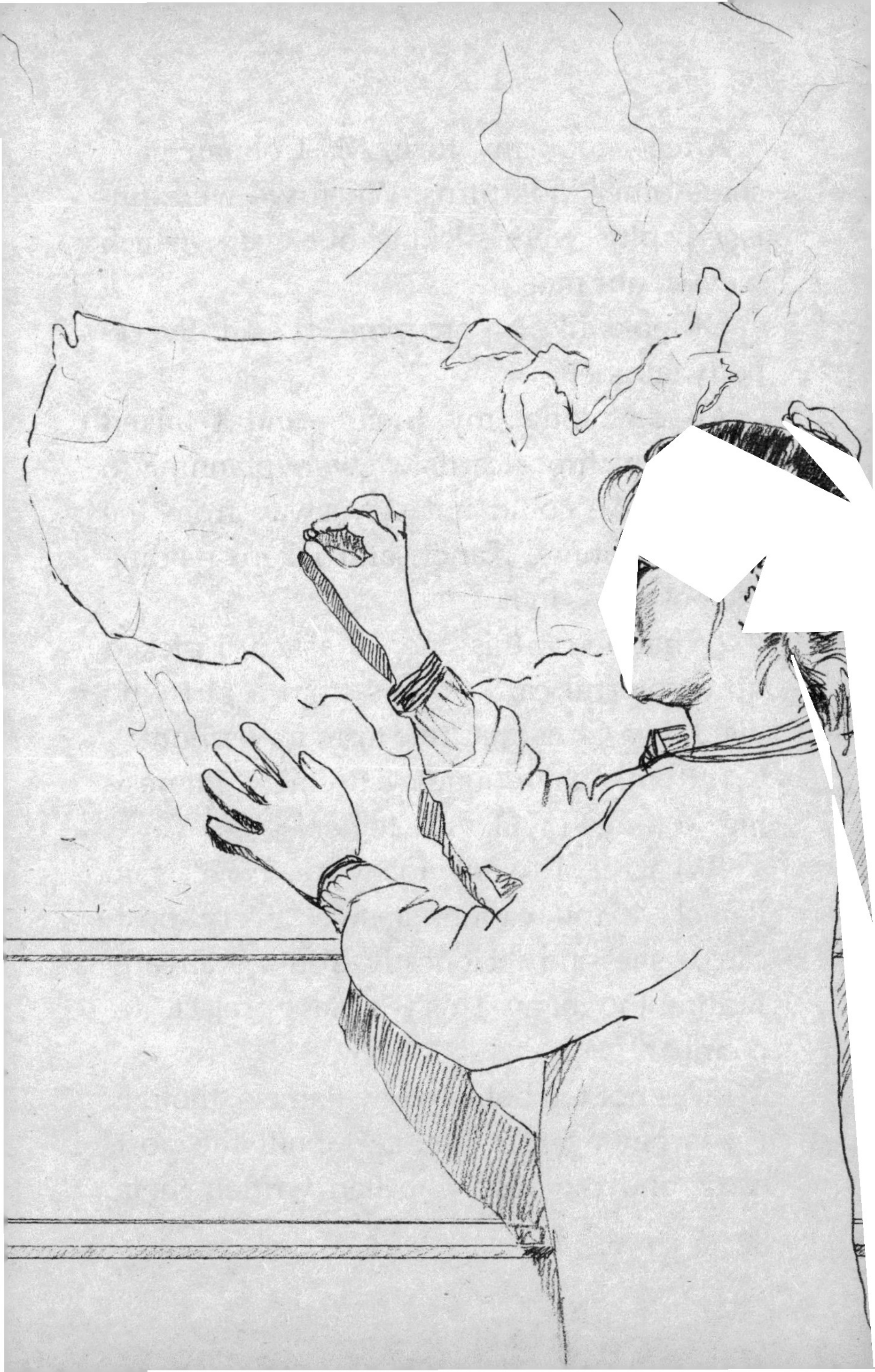

After I took my turn, Ms. Colman gave some other kids turns. When we were finished, pins were sticking out every which way on our map.

"It looks like a porcupine," I said. Everybody laughed.

All day long, my friends and I talked about which postcards we were planning to answer. We could not stay away from the basket. Hannie, Nancy, and I kept reading the postcards in it.

"What about this one?" I asked. I picked up a colorful card. It was from a girl who lived on a Christmas tree farm in Vermont.

"I think she sounds extremely interesting," I said. "I will write to her."

"What if I want to write her?" said Pamela. "You cannot answer every postcard," she said. "Honestly. You are already writing too many. This is a class project. Remember?"

I was not too bothered by Pamela, though. I was having fun thinking about the postcards and the kids who had written them.

Hmm. That gave me an idea. Maybe everyone in my class would forget about stamps for awhile. Maybe that would give me time to work on my collection and make it better. After all, postcards were fun, but I still needed stamps.

"Hey, here is a good postcard," I said. "It is from a boy who likes to collect butterflies."

"Really?" said Nancy. "Let me see."

I could not wait until Postcard Day. And now there was only one more day to go.

Postcard Day

On Postcard Day I woke up bright and early. I gobbled my breakfast, then grabbed my backpack to run to the bus. Elizabeth looked at the clock.

"You are a little early today," she said. "The bus will not be here for another fifteen minutes."

"That is okay," I said.

I was very excited. The night before, I had counted up the number of kids I wanted to write to. I had a full day ahead of me.

Postcard Day started out being lots of fun.

We spent all morning writing our letters. Some kids even decorated theirs.

"Look," said Hannie. "I drew a giraffe on this one."

"That is very nice," I said, "but please do not talk to me while I am writing. I have a lot of cards to answer. And I want to make sure I have time to finish my letters."

By lunchtime I had written a nice stack. I still had plenty more to do, but Ms. Colman told us to put our work away.

"And when you come back from lunch," she said, "I will hand out some math worksheets. We will spend the afternoon working on those."

What? I waved my hand until Ms. Colman called on me. "I thought this was Postcard Day," I said. "What if we have not finished our letters?"

"I did not mean for Postcard Day to be the whole day," replied Ms. Colman. "I think most of your classmates have finished writing their letters by now."

"But I have not."

"Is it possible for you to finish them at home?"

"Maybe," I said. "But what about all the postcards that we have not answered yet?"

"I never expected we would have time to answer them all," said Ms. Colman. "After all, we have over a hundred cards here."

Oh no. This was very bad news.

"I guess you misunderstood, Karen," she said. "I am afraid that this afternoon we need to devote some time to our regular work."

Boo and bullfrogs. Another misunderstanding. I put away my letters and followed my class to the lunchroom. I was certainly getting very good at misunderstandings. It seemed as if I were becoming an expert.

Hannie walked alongside me. She could tell I was not happy.

"Are you upset?" she asked.

"Well, of course I am," I said. "Lots of kids wrote to us. They expected answers.

The ones who do not hear from us will be disappointed."

"The kids who wrote to us were answering a chain letter," said Hannie. "They will not feel bad. They could not be sure that anyone would answer."

That might be true. Still. "I know I would want an answer if I had asked for one," I said.

That afternoon, we worked on our math. It was hard for me to concentrate. I stared at the basket. Lots of cards were still inside. Cards that would not be answered.

How had this happened? How had everything gone so wrong? From the start, the chain letter had been nothing but trouble. First Ms. Colman and my father had gotten angry at me. Then I had gotten into one squabble after another with my classmates. About stamps. Stamps! And now I was disappointing a whole bunch of other kids, kids I had never even met. What a mess.

"Karen," said Ms. Colman. She had noticed me staring at the basket. "Do you need some help with your math?"

"No, thank you," I said. I chewed on my pencil and tried harder to concentrate.

Soon it was time to go home. I put on my sweatshirt and zipped it up. On my way out the door, I stopped at the basket and pulled out a card. It was from a girl who said she was an only child. "How many people do you have in your family?" she had asked.

Now there was a question. It would take me all day to write a letter answering that.

Hank and Bobby walked past me.

"I will trade you this card for that one," said Hank to Bobby.

Stamps again. Hannie tugged at my sleeve.

"Come on," she said. "We do not want to miss the bus."

I dropped the postcard back in the basket and followed my friend out the door.

Surfing the Net

On the way home, I did not feel much like talking. Hannie did, though.

"I have to figure out a way to get more stamps," she said. "I think my collection is the worst in the class."

"Mine is the next worst," I said.

"There must be something we can do."

"No," I said. "I have tried everything. I have asked every person in my family for stamps. I have gone through every old letter I have ever saved. I have written to everyone I know. Nothing is working."

"I'm sure there's something we have not thought of," said Hannie. She drummed her fingers on the seat in front of us. "I know!" she cried.

"What?"

"We can look on the computer. Maybe there is a Web site about stamp collecting. Maybe it would tell us how we could get more stamps."

Well, that was not exactly a way to get stamps. But it was a way to get more ideas.

"When the bus lets us off, I will come to your house," said Hannie. "We will surf the Net."

Hannie held out her arms as if she were balancing on a board. "Surf's up," she said with a grin.

At my house, we asked Nannie if we could use the computer. She sat with us while we worked on-line. We did find a Web site about stamp collecting. Not only that, it was a special Web site just for kids. At the site was a bulletin board where kids could write messages. We read some of them. Hannie looked disappointed.

"These kids all seem to have lots of stamps already," she said. "Nobody seems to have any ideas about how to get more."

I leaned forward and scrolled down the screen. "No," I said. "But there are plenty of kids with lots of things to say."

Hannie placed her fingers on the keyboard.

Help! she typed. *I am stranded on a desert island. Send stamps!*

"If only it was this easy to get mail," she said.

"Wait!" I cried. "It *is* this easy to get mail. Not *mail* mail, but electronic mail."

"What good does that do us? There are no stamps on electronic mail."

"Who cares about stamps?" I said. "Don't you see? This would be the perfect way to answer all the postcards that are still sitting in the basket at school. Our class could start a Web site. It could have a mailbox. That way, we could write back and forth to our new pen pals all the time. It would be fast and easy."

"I was hoping for more stamps," said Hannie.

"Not me," I declared. "I do not care if I never see another stamp as long as I live."

I closed up the computer and shut it off.

I could not wait for school the next day. I could not wait to tell my great idea to the class.

A New Project

I love to start the day with something important to announce to the class. The next morning at school Ms. Colman noticed that I was a little fidgety during attendance.

"Karen," she said, "you look as if there is something you want to share with the class."

"There is," I said. "I figured out how we can answer all the postcards that are left in the basket."

"Oh," said Ms. Colman. "Karen, I thought I made it clear that we would not be able to do that."

"We could start a Web site," I said quickly. I knew Ms. Colman would love my idea once she heard it.

"A Web site," she repeated.

"Yes," I said. "It could be a new club. I even have a name for it, the Postcard Club. But it will not be a regular club. It will be on the Internet. And any kid who wants to can write to us there."

No one in my class said a word. Maybe they had not understood me.

"Okay," I said. Someone needed to start the ball rolling. "What we need to do is write a letter. We can print out lots of copies and send it out to all the kids who wrote postcards to us."

Ms. Colman laughed. "I think you are getting a little ahead of us here, Karen," she said. "This is a big project, one we need to talk about first. Does anyone have any questions?"

"I do," said Natalie. "How can other kids write to us on a Web site?"

"It will have a mailbox," I explained. "Kids can leave messages there, and we can read them and send messages back."

"But what would the rest of the Web site be?" asked Ricky.

"That is a good question," said Ms. Colman. She took out a large sheet of paper and a Magic Marker. "What information would you like to have on a Web site?"

"Information about our class," said Nancy. "So other kids could get to know us."

"Good idea," said Ms. Colman.

At the top of the page she wrote a heading. *Our Web site,* it said.

"And what information would you like to include?" she asked.

"Our grade," said Natalie.

"Our pets," said Ricky.

"Our favorite books," said Sara.

"Our hobbies," said Bobby.

Hobbies? I knew what that meant. I groaned.

"Anything else?" asked Ms. Colman.

Hannie raised her hand. "What stamps we need," she said.

Even I had to laugh at that.

Soon we had a long list of information we wanted to include. Ms. Colman read it out loud.

"This will be a good project for us," she said. "But before we begin, I need to do a little investigating myself. I need to find out if it is possible for us to set up a Web site, and how we would go about doing that."

"You could ask Mr. Baker," suggested Nancy. Mr. Baker is one of the teachers in our school. He knows all about computers.

"That would be a smart place to start," said Ms. Colman. "Maybe he could help us set up the Web site himself. Now," she said, "we need to get on with the work we have scheduled for today."

"Excuse me!" I raised my hand. "We still need to write the letter," I reminded her. "The one announcing the club."

Ms. Colman glanced at the clock. "Karen," she said thoughtfully, "would you like to write a draft of the letter yourself? You could bring it into class tomorrow, and then we could make time to work on it together."

"Yes," I said. I am very good at writing letters. Ms. Colman had picked the perfect person for the job.

The Postcard Club

At last our Web site was ready. Mr. Baker knew all about Web sites. He helped Ms. Colman set up ours. The Postcard Club had lots of information about our class. We even decided to write poems and include them. I wrote a funny poem about my brother Andrew.

The class liked the form letter I brought in. That is, they liked most of it. Ms. Colman was not so sure about one part, the part where I pointed out that the Web site was my idea. "Do you think it is necessary to say that, Karen?" she asked.

"I do," I said. "Because it shows that kids can have ideas. I had an idea, I told it to you, and you helped us turn it into a class project. Now everyone who reads the letter will know how special our class is."

Ms. Colman laughed. "All right," she said. "You win. Overall, you have done a very good and thorough job."

That afternoon, we mailed the letter. We sent a copy to every single kid who had sent us a postcard with his or her address. Our letter told our new friends how to find our Web site. And it told them they could contact us by sending electronic mail to our mailbox. Now all we had to do was sit back and wait for the messages to pour in.

I knew it would take time for our letter to reach our new pen pals. So I knew there would not be any notes on our Web site yet. Still, I checked every day. But by the end of that week, we had not received any mail. Luckily, I could use our home computer to check the mailbox on our Web site. Nope. No messages yet. I reread the poem I had written.

MY BROTHER ANDREW
by Karen B.

Andrew is my little brother.
He is simply like no other!

He collects big trucks with cranes,
Racing cars and planes and trains.
Sometimes he puts bugs in jars.
I think he is quite bizarre!

Still, I love to play with him,
Bike and skate and sled and swim.
Did I say he moved away?
Andrew, please come back to play!

No doubt about it, my poem was the best in the class. I hoped my classmates would not be upset if all our new pen pals addressed their messages specifically to me.

On Monday morning, first thing, I asked Ms. Colman if I could go to our Web site and check our mailbox. She said that we needed to do some things before that. First we had to take attendance. Bor-ing. Then we had to show her the books we had chosen for independent reading. Then we had to start reading one of them. Usually I love to read. But that day, I just sat there staring at the same blurry page. Ms. Colman walked past me and noticed.

"All right, Karen," she said. "Maybe it is time to visit our Web site and check our mail."

Hurray! *Bing.* I turned on the computer. *Click.* I opened our mailbox.

Oh, goody, there were messages. "Mail!" I cried out. Everyone gathered around to see.

One thing surprised me. None of the messages mentioned me specifically. Oh well. What they did mention — every single message — was stamp collecting. That is because most of the kids in our class had listed it as their hobby.

One of the messages asked about the best way to remove stamps from envelopes.

Nancy pushed her way closer to the computer. "I will answer that one," she volunteered.

Another message was from a kid who said that she had bought some stamp trading cards at the post office.

"Wow," said Hank. "I want to talk to her."

We were very busy answering our mail. I did not even mind that all the kids who wrote were writing messages about stamp collecting. After all, it was fun to read mail from so many kids.

A Brand-new Pen Pal

And that is how our class started the Postcard Club. After that, we spent some time every day answering our mail. Our class is always very, very busy.

One day I was sitting next to Hannie again, during silent reading time. We were sunk into the big, fluffy pillows. Hannie nudged me. "I wish I had a teapot dress like that," she said. "She really does have the coolest clothes."

I looked up. There was Ms. Agna again. I

was surprised to see her. Postcards had stopped pouring in for me, and she had not visited our room in more than a week. I figured that by now I had received all the postcards I was going to get.

This time, Ms. Agna did not have a big bag of cards. She had only one. She smiled at me from across the room and handed the card to Ms. Colman.

"Well," said Ms. Colman as she looked it over, "this is quite exciting. Karen, please come up and show the class the card you received. We will have to add a new push pin to our map. In fact, we will have to add a whole new section to our map."

Ms. Colman handed me the card. Oh, my goodness, the card had come all the way from Australia! That must be why it had taken so long to arrive. I read it aloud to the class.

Hi, it said. *I am writing from Sydney, which is the largest city in Australia. I have lots of hobbies, but my favorite is the computer. Please write back. Your friend, Alexander McCully.*

"What does the stamp look like?" asked Pamela.

Uh-oh. The stamp. I wondered if Ms. Colman would let me keep it. It was not a kangaroo stamp, but it was very cool. I certainly did not want to give it to Pamela. Ms. Colman must have guessed what I was thinking.

"It is very special to receive mail all the way from Australia," she said. "So special that, this time, Karen, I think you may keep the stamp as well as the postcard." Phew! "And you ought to mail Alexander one of our letters announcing the Postcard Club," Ms. Colman continued. "If his hobby is computers, he is probably on-line."

Yippee! At last it was my lucky day. At last I had the good luck I had been waiting for all along.

"Pass the postcard around," said Nancy.

"Okay," I said. "But please do not smudge the stamp."

A stamp from Australia. I would have to make a beautiful new page in my album for that. But even more important, I could not wait to write to Alexander. I had so many questions to ask. Were there kangaroos in Sydney? What was the weather like in Australia?

Now I had a brand-new pen pal from all the way around the world. And when Alexander found out about the Postcard Club, he and I would be able to leave messages for each other every single day.

L. GODWIN

About the Author

Ann M. Martin lives in New York City and loves animals, especially cats. She has two cats of her own, Gussie and Woody.

Other books by Ann M. Martin that you might enjoy are *Stage Fright*; *Me and Katie (the Pest)*; and the books in *The Baby-sitters Club* series.

Ann likes ice cream and *I Love Lucy*. And she has her own little sister, whose name is Jane.

Don't Miss #102

KAREN'S BLACK CAT

Elizabeth called the first number, but all the kittens had been adopted already.

"I knew we should have called first thing in the morning!" I said.

Elizabeth called the second number. When she finished, she gave us the thumbs-up sign.

"The woman who put in the ad is Mrs. Cooper. She just got home from work and our call was the first one she answered," she said when she hung up the phone. "We can go see the kittens in the morning."

I could hardly wait! I counted kittens to fall asleep.

I saw them in my dreams at night. I saw them in my cereal bowl in the morning.

At nine o'clock on Saturday, we drove

over to see the litter. Thank goodness!

"Look how cute they are!" I said.

There were six kittens in a box. Four were gray. One was black. And yippee! One was the orange tiger-striped kitten I had been hoping for!

"We will call you Pumpkin!" I said as if I had just thought of it.

I picked up the striped kitten and held him to my cheek. His paws were so tiny and his eyes were so big.

"Look, he is the cutest of all," I said.

But no one was looking at Pumpkin. Everyone was in a circle around Kristy. She was holding another one of the kittens. It was the black one.

"She is friendly and playful," I heard Daddy say.

The next thing I knew, Daddy was taking a vote.

"Whoever votes for the black kitten, say 'Aye,' " he said.

There were seven "Ayes" and one "me."

"We will take this black kitten," said Daddy.